The Adventures of Mr Toad

A. Hides

Dedicated to Anthony John Hides

CONTENTS

Chapter 1 1

Chapter 2 5

Chapter 3 12

Chapter 4 23

Chapter 5 31

ACKNOWLEDGMENTS

This story was written by the late Anthony John Hides, who's love for the Wind In The Willows stories inspired this book.

Chapter 1

It was a fine spring morning on the Riverbank and Rat and Mole were up early as usual.

They had finished their chores, had breakfast and were sitting on the veranda sipping tea.

"Don't you think the River's looking splendid at this time of year, Mole?" said Rat, reaching forward to refill his cup.

"Absolutely," said Mole. "I love the River almost as much as you do, Rattie." They sat for some moments in silence, each busy with their own thoughts. "Now that you have finished painting the boat," said Mole, "Do you think we could have lunch on the River today?"

Rat turned and smiled fondly at him. "Of course we can, Molie. Of course we can."

Rat said he had some adjustments to make to the boat's new rowlocks and made his way to the boathouse. *Dear old Mole*, though Rat. *He so enjoys picnics and I can never say no to him.*

Mole, meanwhile, had returned to the kitchen to brew a fresh pot of tea, and while waiting for the kettle to boil began packing the hamper. When the tea was ready he carried it out onto the veranda and called to Rat and placed the tray on the table.

Rat turned and said to Mole, "That didn't take long. It's all ready now, Mole." Then he sat down and helped himself to some more tea.

When they had finished their tea Mole returned to the kitchen to finish packing the hamper and Rat went to get the boat out. He pushed the boat to the end of the landing stage and awaited the arrival of Mole.

As Mole came down the path carrying the hamper,

he called to Rat, "I hope I have packed enough, Rattie."

To which Rat replied, "Well there are only the two of us, Mole, so hop in and we will shove off."

Mole secured the hamper and climbed aboard. Then Rat eased the boat gently into midstream. Mole then took up the oars and began to row. Under Rat's tuition he had become quite an expert in the art of rowing and learned to know the ways of the river almost as well as Rat.

As they approached the bridge that led to Toad Hall, Mole said to Rat, "Where do you want to stop, Rattie, the knoll or the pasture beyond the bridge?

"The knoll, I think, then we can sit beneath that big oak tree," said Rat. They moored the boat to the grassy bank and carried the hamper ashore. Rat spread the rug on the grass while Mole unpacked the hamper.

"What's in the hamper?" said Rat, squatting on the grass beside Mole.

"There is cold meat, salad, tomatoes, ham sandwiches, sausage rolls, and some of my fresh-baked scones and fruit preserve, plus a few bottles of ginger beer."

"A feast fit for a king – I don't know how you do it, Molie."

After they had eaten their fill, Rat stretched out

on the grass to have a nap, while Mole took a stroll along the towpath to stretch his legs. He came to the fork in the path which led to Wild Wood and saw a familiar figure coming towards him.

It was Badger, and as he got closer, he called, "Hello Mole, is Rat with you?"

"Yes, he's asleep back there," said Mole. "We were having a picnic."

Badger laughed and said, "That accounts for it, but I can't stop, Mole, I have to go and see Toad, he sent me a message to go round and see him as soon as possible. I'm sorry to have missed Rat, but I will catch up with you both later."

Mole went back to Rat and found him awake and told him of his encounter with Badger.

"Curiouser and curiouser," said Rat.

Rat and Mole repacked the picnic hamper and made preparations for the journey home. As they glided silently through the water, Rat said to Mole, "I wonder what old Toad has been up to now."

To which Mole replied, "Your guess is as good as mine, Rattie, especially where Toad is concerned."

Chapter 2

After leaving Mole, Badger crossed the bridge and took the lane that led to Toad Hall. As he approached the Hall he spotted two young weasels skulking in the bushes.

Loathsome creatures, thought Badger. *Nothing but trouble.*

"Good day, Mr Badger," the squeaked. "Nice day for a stroll."

"Hmph," said Badger, and went on his way.

A huge wall surrounded Toad's Estate, with a huge iron gate set in it, beyond which a gravel drive some hundred yards long led up to the front of the house. As he walked up the drive towards the house, he kept running Toad's message over in his mind. For some reason he was perturbed.

He arrived at the front door and rang the bell. The door was opened almost immediately by Toad.

"Thank goodness you've come, Badger," said Toad. "I'm at my wits' end."

Badger thought Toad looked very distraught and said, "What exactly is the problem, my friend?"

Toad looked pitifully at Badger and said, "It's her, she is coming here, and there is nothing I can do."

"Calm down, Toad," said Badger. "And start from the beginning. Right now you are not making much sense."

"It all started two days ago," said Toad. "I had a letter from her."

Badger said, "Who is 'her'?"

And Toad said, "Florence, she is a distant cousin from up north, a branch of the family we don't have much to do with. They are not very well off, you see, and never amounted to much, so you can imagine my consternation when she announced her intention of coming here for a visit."

Badger said, "What is so terrible about that?"

Toad moaned. "You don't know her. She is an ogre, and will impose her authority on this place, and it will never be the same again, and I will be reduced to some sort of lackey. Oh woe is me."

"Can't you write and put her off?" said Badger.

"Too late," said Toad. "She will be here the day after tomorrow and once she is here I will never get rid of her." He began hopping around the room in anguish. "It's the end of the road for Toad," he cried.

"Calm down, Toad," said Badger. "You will give yourself a heart attack if you are not careful."

"Then think of something. I really can't go on like this."

Badger told Toad he would go and see Rat and Mole and together maybe they would come up with something. "In the meantime, Toad," he said. "I want you to take a sedative and go to bed."

Toad said, "Thank you Badger, I think I will."

It was early evening when Badger arrived at Rat's place. He knocked and the door was opened by Mole.

"Hello Badger," he said. "Come in, we were just about to have out tea. Won't you join us?" "Hello you two," he said. "Yes, I'd love to, thank you, Mole." And he sat down at the table.

"How did the meeting with Toad go?" said Rat.

While they were having tea, he related the whole story to them.

"Goodness me," said Mole. "Poor old Toad."

Rat said, "Under normal circumstances I would suggest extreme caution as it is really a family matter, and we have no right to interfere. But as Toad himself has asked four our help we are duty bound to help any way we can."

"He is our friend and needs our help," said Badger.

"We must put our heads together and think of something," said Mole. The three of them were lost in thought for a long time. Suddenly, Mole spoke. "It seems to me that our best tactic is to somehow cause this cousin of Toad's to leave of her own free will."

"That's not a bad idea," said Badger. "Of course we will have to get to know her better in order to formulate a workable plan."

Rat suggested they put the idea to Toad. "After all," said Rat, "If we adopt this plan, he will have to play his part." Rat then said, "We will go and see Toad tomorrow and if he agrees, we can put the plan into effect."

Badger then said, "I think it would be a good idea to ask him if she has any particular aversions, because most females have an aversion to something or other."

As the hour was now so late, Rat suggested Badger stay the night. "You can use the guest room, it's far too late for you to walk home to Wild Wood at this time of night." Badger said, "Thank you, Rattie, I accept. It is a rather long walk home." Mole went up to prepare Badger's bed.

"Well we have made progress tonight, I think," said Rat. "Now I suggest that we retire to bed."

Mole came down and said to Badger, "Your bed is ready, Badger."

He said, "Thank you, Mole," then wished them both goodnight and went up to bed, and Rat and Mole followed soon after.

As usual Mole was up and about first the next morning and busy preparing breakfast. Rat and Badger came down together.

"Good morning, Mole," they said.

"My, that smells good," said Badger.

"Then sit down and eat," said Mole, which they were only too glad to do. When breakfast was over, they went over the plan again.

"You know," said Rat. "We only have Toad's word concerning this cousin of his and you know he can exaggerate at times."

"Yes, Rattie, but we won't be sure until she arrives,

and in the meantime we'll carry on as planned and say nothing about our doubts to Toad."

Toad, as usual, was pleased to see them, and ushered them into the lounge.

"I am so pleased to see you fellows. I assume Badger has informed you about the predicament I am in?"

"Yes," said Rattie. "And after a lot of thought, have come up with a plan that might work." He related to Toad their discussion the previous night and how they planned to deal with the situation.

He listened attentively, then he said, "Oh joy, I knew you fellows would think of something. It's a splendid idea." He paused, then said, "There is only one snag – I can't think of anything she is averse to. Nothing comes to mind."

"Don't worry," said Rat. "There has to be something. Now as I understand it, she will be here tomorrow, so we will be up early to be here when she arrives, then you can introduce us to her."

Before they took their leave, Mole said to Toad, "Now remember, act normally and don't do anything to arouse her suspicions." He gave them his promise.

"Right," said Rat. "We will see you in the morning." Then they left.

On leaving Toad Hall, they decided to call in on Badger, to give him an update on the situation. Mole was always uneasy venturing to Wild Wood on account of the stoats and weasels. It wasn't too bad in the daylight, but you would not get him near the place after dark.

It was alright for Badger, he lived here and, being a big fellow, no-one messed with him.

Badger's front door was within a dense thicket, and was made of solid oak, and the heavy door knocker made a deep, hollow sound.

"Ah, Rat and Mole," he said. "Come in, come in." he indicated his cudgel as he laid it down.

"You can't be too careful round here," he said.

They told him about their visit to Toad and how glad he was that they had come up with a plan.

"Good," said Badger. "Now, my friends, you have to realise that this whole scheme rests on our estimation of this cousin of his, so first we have to meet her and decide whether Toad's fears are justified, and when we meet tomorrow we'll have a clearer idea of what she is really like."

Rat said, "Fair enough, Badger."

They arranged to meet at the river bridge at nine o'clock the following morning and go to Toad Hall together.

Chapter 3

Rat and Mole arrived at the bridge just before nine o'clock and found Badger already there.

"Good morning, fellow conspirators," he called.

"Good morning, Badger," they replied.

Badger said, "Today's the day, eh?" Then they set

off down the lane. When they got to the tall iron gate they saw Toad standing in the porch. They pushed open the gates and started to walk up the drive.

"Toad's pointing at something," said Rat. Then they heard a car behind them. It was a taxi, and it was coming up the drive. As it passed them, they caught a glimpse of the passenger, and by the look of her dress it was clearly a female, but it was the face that caught their attention, it was full of malice before it looked away.

"It would seem cousin Florence has arrived," said Badger.

Poor Toad was lugging cases from the taxi as they arrived, while she stood by and watched.

"Could you lend a hand please, fellow, these cases are awfully heavy," Toad wailed.

Between them, they carried the cases into the hallway. There were six of them.

"Thank you," said Toad. "May I introduce you to my cousin Florence from up north.

Florence, these three gentlemen are particular friends of mine – Mr Badger, Mr Rat, and Mr Mole."

They held out their hands and said, "Pleased to meet you."

She made no response, but turned and marched into the house. Then, turning to Toad, she said,

"Where is my room, Toad?"

To which he replied, "At the top of the stairs, facing you."

Then she said, "Arrange for my luggage to be brought up," and marched off up the stairs to her room. The three of them were again called upon to act as porters, and carried the cases up to her room and left them just inside the door, which she closed and locked. Whereupon they quickly made their escape.

"I am so sorry about that," said Toad.

"Most rude if you ask me," said Badger. "But at least we now know what we are up against." As they moved towards the door, Badger said to Toad, "We need to talk, Toad, and it is obvious we can't talk here. We should go somewhere quiet and discuss the situation."

"We can go to my place, it's nearest," said Rat. Everyone agreed and a short time later they were on their way.

"It will not be a bad thing if she discovers that you have gone out," said Badger. As it will go some way to impress on her that you are a free agent, and can come and go and you please." There was general agreement on that.

When they got to Rat's house, Mole busied about making lunch and asked Rat to lay the table. "We have nothing special today, so it will not be long."

Rat began to put the plates and cutlery on the table while lunch was being prepared. Mole carried in a large tray and returned to fetch another.

Badger said, "My, my, a fine spread. You never fail to amaze me, Mole."

Rat said, "That's Mole for you."

"Mole looked a little embarrassed and said, "Oh, they're just some leftovers from our picnic," but Rat knew better.

It was a pleasant meal and Toad seemed a lot more like his old self. When the meal was over, the table was cleared and they settled themselves comfortable. Rat handed round the coffee, and the serious business began.

"Before we start," said Badger. "A thought occurred to me that I think I ought to mention." He paused. "Now, Toad," he said. "Apart from the one on your chain, how many front door keys have you got?"

Toad said, "Two, this one, plus a spare."

Badger then said, "And where do you keep this spare key?" "In the kitchen drawer," said Toad.

Badger said, "Then remove it and keep it on your person or give it to someone for safekeeping."

"Why is that?" asked Toad.

"Because if she finds it, she may take it into her

head to have a duplicate made and that's the last thing you want."

Toad looked aghast. "Good God, you're right," said Toad. "I'll remove it as soon as I get home and I would be grateful if you would keep it for me, Badger."

"Of course I will, old fellow," said Badger. "And while you're at it, Toad, remove the keys to the other outside doors, just in case." Their discussion centred on their first impressions of Florence,and on that they were all agreed, not very good.

Toad said, "When she told me she was coming, she said it would be for a few days, then turns up with those cases."

Badger then cut in. "The same thought occurred to me and it seems clear to me that she intends to stay a lot longer than that, maybe even for good."

Toad moaned. "Oh no, I couldn't stand it. We have to do something, Badger. I did tell you what she was like."

Rat said, "Don't go on so, Toad, we are doing our best to help, but it may take a bit of time."

Badger said, "I think you had better get back and retrieve those keys, Toad, before she gets her hands on them. There is little more we can do for the time being."

"I'll row you up to the bridge," said Rat. "It will be

quicker than walking." He got the boat out and Toad hopped in. When they got to the bridge, Toad leapt out.

"Thanks Rattie," he called, then ran off.

When Rat got back, Badger had already gone home.

"What do you make of all this business, Molie?" said Rat.

"I think Badger is right, Rattie, this Florence intended to stay – the question is, for how long?"

Rat thought for a moment, then said, "At the moment it is anybody's guess, but we have to do everything we can to help dear Toad."

The following morning, Rat was up before Mole for once and went for an early stroll along the river path in the direction of the bridge. When he reached the bridge, he paused to watch a family of ducks swimming by, when he heard his name called, and on turning, saw Toad running down the lane towards him.

"Rattie," he shouted. "The key has gone. She must have taken it."

"Badger must be told immediately," said Rat. "He was expecting something like this to happen." Rat said that as they were now quite close to Wild Wood they should go to Badger's and tell him what had happened – he would know what to do.

When Badger opened the door and saw Rat and Toad standing there, he surmised that something was wrong.

"What has happened?" he said.

"The key has gone," said Toad. "He must have it."

"Ah, I half expected as much. She has shown her hand at last."

Toad was very agitated and said, "What are we going to do now?"

"It is quite simple," said Badger. "We change the lock." Toad said that he had never done that before.

"Well I have," said Badger. "It is quite an easy job, as long as the new lock is the same pattern as the old one."

"Now I come to think of it," said Toad. "A new lock was fitted to that door about two years ago."

Badger said, "Well there you are then, if the same locksmith fitted that lock, he will know the pattern."

Rat suggested to Toad that he should go to the village locksmith as soon as possible and get a new lock. Badger agreed. So Toad immediately set off to the village.

Badger made them both coffee and they sat in Badger's comfortable old armchairs and chatted. After a while, Badger said, "Won't Mole be wondering where you are?"

"By Jove, you're right," said Rat. "I had better be on my way." He thanked Badger for the coffee and rose to leave when there was a knock at the door, and opened it to admit Mole.

"Come in, Mole," said Badger. "We were just discussing the latest developments." He proceeded to tell Mole the events that had occurred when Rat went for his early walk.

He listened attentively and then said, "She can't have had time to get another key made, it's only just nine o'clock and there is the possibility that she will run into Toad." Badger said that he had not considered that possibility, and that in such an event, he would have the sense to keep his head down.

Toad came in looking excited. "Oh Badger," he said. "You should have been there, he recognised me as soon as I walked in, but then he would, wouldn't he? Then he asked me what I wanted, and when I told him about the lock he said, 'Do you mean the one I fitted two years ago at the Hall?' I said it was, and he produced an exact duplicate." Toad then assumed the pose of a conspirator and his chest swelled. He said, "Then he tried to catch me out. He asked me what was wrong with the old one – that's when I had to box clever – so I simply said I had lost the key." Now, everyone was smiling, Toad most of all.

"Let me see the lock, Toad," said Badger, and Toad produced it with a flourish.

"It comes with three keys," said Toad.

Badger examined the lock closely and said, "Well done, Toad, now what about those other keys I asked you to get hold of?"

Toad replied, "They are in my pocket, Badger," and handed them to Badger for safekeeping.

"What tools will you need to do the job, Badger?" said Rat.

"Just a screwdriver should be sufficient, I think, but just in case I will also take a chisel."

"We now have to choose the right moment," said Rat.

Badger replied, "If Florence has gone to the village, then now might be as good a time as any." Then he went to his shed and collected his tools. "Come along, Toad, we will attempt to change those locks, if the coast is clear."

Rat said that he and Mole would return home, and they arranged to all meet at his house later that day.

Badger said, "Fair enough, Rattie," then they all left together.

When Badger and Toad arrived at Toad Hall, they found the gates wide open, and waiting at the top of the drive was a taxi.

"She must be going out," said Toad. Then the door opened and she came out and got in the taxi just as Toad and Badger walked up the drive.

Badger said to Toad, "She has probably gone to the village, and it is almost certain that she'll get another key cut."

When they reached the house, Badger examined the lock and said, "This will not take long and in any case, we have plenty of time," then set to work.

It did not take him very long to remove the old lock and it a new one, and Toad commented that no-one would ever know.

Badger replied, "That is the general idea." He then tested the lock of the door three times and said, "That's it, Toad, and now to take the one off your chain and put this new one on it, and I'll take the two spare ones home with me." They cleaned up and went into the house, and Toad made them both a cup of coffee.

"I will hang on to this old lock for you, Toad. It may come in handy."

"What happens when she comes back and finds her key won't fit?" said Toad.

"Nothing. She will just assume that she picked up the wrong key," said Badger. "I will be off to Rattie's soon," said Badger. "If she fails to return within two hours, then make your way to Rat's house." Then he took his leave.

Toad sat in an armchair in the lounge to await developments. He chose a seat near the door so as not to miss a sound. After an hour, he heard a metallic sort of clicking noise, then it came again. There was silence for a moment, then the doorbell rang. He opened the door to find Florence standing there surrounded by packages. She looked furious, but said nothing, she just scooped up her shopping and marched in, then went straight up to her room. Toad made his escape and set off to Rat's house.

Chapter 4

All four friends were seated comfortably in Rat's lounge, drinking coffee and sampling Mole's homemade scones. Badger suggested they run through events so far, and asked Toad if he had anything to report.

"Oh I have indeed," said Toad, and he related the

behaviour of Florence when she found her key would not fit the lock, and her look of fury at being thwarted. Toad's recital met with approval all round, and he looked very pleased with himself.

"So she has no idea that the lock has been changed?" said Badger.

"Not an inkling," said Toad.

"We now have to consider our next move," said Badger. They were silent for a long time, deep in thought, then Toad broke the silence.

"I wonder what she would do if she was confronted by a weasel." And they all laughed out loud.

Badger said, "Toad, you are a genius, why that's it: we enlist the help of the weasels."

Rat said, "Are you serious, Badger? They would laugh at us. We have always had trouble with them and the stoats. It's unthinkable."

Badger said, "Not if there was something in it for them. You know weasels as well as I do,

Rattie."

Rat replied, "Maybe, but the weasels, Badger, I mean to say."

Badger tried a different approach. "Now think about it for a moment. It would not be our doing at all. Don't you see, we can't be blamed whatever happens."

Rat wasn't quite convinced, and said, "It's true they would do anything for a profit, but are you really sure really sure about this, Badger?" "Absolutely," he said. "What do you think, Mole?" "All I know is that they frighten me," he said.

"They frighten me, too," said Toad. "But I think the scheme could work."

Rat then said, "Alright, let's hear this idea of yours."

"It is simple. We negotiate a deal with the weasels, whereby they scare her enough to want to leave, in return for a certain amount of money."

"And what did you have in mind to give them for doing this?" said Rat.

Badger said, "Well I hadn't thought that far ahead, but shall we say twenty pounds?"

"Twenty pounds?" cried Rat. "They would kill their own mothers for that sort of money." Badger said he was open to any other suggestions, and asked the others what they thought.

Toad said he liked the sound of it, and Mole was inclined to agree, providing he was not expected to go into Wild Wood and negotiate.

"What about you, Rattie?"

"Alright, count me in," he said.

Badger said that all they had to do now was to work out the details. "Perhaps we should put the plan to the weasels first. Maybe they will have some ideas on the subject." "They are pretty good at that sort of thing," said Mole.

Badger said he would go to the weasels and put the proposition to them and try to gauge their reactions and also consider any ideas they may have – assuming they were interested.

"They have a healthy respect for you, Badger, and I am sure they will listen to what you have to say," said Rat.

The party then broke up, and they went their separate ways. Badger said he would go to see the weasels in the morning, then he and Toad said goodbye to Rat and Mole and went home.

In the morning, Badger set out from his house in Wild Wood. He knew where to find the den of the weasels and it was not too far away. In the heart of the wood was an old, hollow oak tree, and inside the trunk was a tunnel that led to the weasels' den. Badger had known about it for a long time and they were aware that he knew, but he never bothered them, and they afforded him the same respect.

When Badger came to the hollow tree, he raised his cudgel and gave the trunk a few hefty blows. It was not long before a shrivelled visage appeared above the trunk.

"Ah, Mr Badger," squeaked a thin voice. "To what do we owe the pleasure of your company this fine morning?"

"I have a proposition, to our mutual benefit, that you may be interested in," said Badger.

"In that case you had better come in," said the weasel, so Badger climbed up the trunk and dropped down into the tunnel. It was a tight squeeze for Badger, but he managed to get through. There were small rooms leading off from the tunnel on each side, but his guide led him straight on until they came to a larger room at the very end of the main tunnel.

This turned out to be the private room of the chief weasel, who looked hard at Badger and said, "What can I do for you, Mr Badger?"

"Help me out with a small problem," said Badger, and proceeded to explain the reason for his visit.

Badger had been the guest of the weasels for two hours or more by the time he emerged from the tunnel, but he had accomplished his mission and hurried off to tell the others. He went first to tell Rat and Mole.

"Well done, Badger," said Rat, but Mole got really carried away.

"You actually went down their hole, Badger? Oh how brave of you, only you could have carried that off," he said. Badger told them that the weasels had suggested a plan that he approved of only on the understanding that she was not to be harmed in any way.

"What is this plan?" said Rat.

Badger replied that it required the involvement of Toad, and would take the form of a haunting of sorts, late at night, after she had retired to bed. Naturally, Toad would be a major player in the game. Just then there came a knock at the door, and when Rat answered it, Toad bounced in.

"Hello, you fellows," he said. "What is the latest news?"

"Hello Toad," they replied, and while Mole was making the coffee, they brought Toad up to date on events so far.

"The only thing required from you now, Toad, is the exact floor plan of Toad Hall," said Badger. he then said that he would take Toad's map to the weasels the next morning. Mole then served the coffee, and suggested that they both stay for lunch "How much did you offer them for their services?" said Rat.

Badger thought for a moment, then said, "I didn't offer them money as such. Instead, I told them we would stock their larder with enough provisions to last them through the summer months, which I estimate would cost about twenty pounds."

"That sounds reasonable, and I can also throw in some bottles from my wine cellar."

While Rat and Mole were preparing lunch, Toad

and Badger discussed the coming event, and Badger said that he hoped they had not overlooked anything.

"By the way," said Toad. "Did they say when this shindig was going to start?"

Badger replied, "No, but I will be seeing them in the morning when I take the map over and I will tell them that we need plenty of notice, as I want to be there, in order to see fair play and that my conditions are complied with."

Toad looked surprised, and said to him, "Are you really going to be there, Badger?"

"Yes, but only as an observer and I will be well out of sight. Perhaps Rat or Mole would like to join me." Rat then called them into lunch.

During lunch, which was a very pleasant one, Rat remarked that he could not help overhearing that Badger intended to be present when the operations at Toad Hall began, and told Badger that he and Mole would like to join him.

"Of course, old fellow, I would be delighted, so long as you both understand that as we must remain undercover, it could be a bit uncomfortable." Mole said that he would make a couple of thermos flasks and a bite to eat as well as some warm rugs to keep them warm.

The rest of the evening went very well, and there were all in a happy mood. Badger said that as it was getting late, he should be going. Toad said that he also should make a move and told them he would see them in the morning. They thanked Rat and Mole for the meal, and wished them goodnight. Then they left together and set off along the path towards the bridge.

"You know, Mole," said Rat. "Although I agreed to go along with this plan, I still have my doubts."

Mole said, "Badger knows what he's doing, Rattie, after all he knows the weasels better than anyone, and I do not think they will let him down. They wouldn't dare."

Chapter 5

When Toad arrived home that evening, there was no sign of Florence. *She has probably just shut herself in her room*, thought Toad, and went into the lounge, where he poured himself a large drink then settled into his armchair. He had been on the go for much of the day and felt quite weary, and it was not long before he fell asleep. He was woken by the ringing of a bell, and, opening his eyes, saw that it was nearly dark. The bell was still ringing and he realised it was the doorbell, and went to answer it. Florence stood there and was shaking with rage.

"I have been trying to get in for more than an hour," she ranted. "Where on earth have you been?"

Toad could only mumble, "I'm sorry, I nodded off in the chair."

She pushed Toad aside and stepped into the hall, saying, "Never mind all that. I shouldn't have to wait on the doorstep till you decide to open the door. It's not good enough, Toad, so I insist that you give me a key to the front door, and don't only mumble something about arranging to get one cut," she said, and flounced off to her room.

Oh dear, thought Toad. *She is even worse than I imagined she would be*, but consoled himself with the thought that if Badger's plan worked, it would soon be all over.

The next morning it was raining hard, and when Toad went to the kitchen to prepare his breakfast, he saw no sign of her, for which he was thankful. Sitting at the table eating bacon and eggs, Toad heard the doorbell ring, and on opening the door he beheld Mole, standing beneath a large umbrella.

"Do come out of the rain, Mole," he said, and Mole shook the umbrella and stepped inside.

"I can't stay," he said. "I just came to tell you that we have heard from Badger and the message is, tonight's the night."

"Oh goody, I can hardly wait," said Toad.

"Badger said you were not to be alarmed by anything you see or hear after it gets dark.

Now I must be off," said Mole.

Toad saw his friend to the door and said, "Thank you, Mole, thank you all."

Mole nodded and scuttled off down the drive. When Toad had closed the door, it took all his self-control to prevent himself from shouting 'whoopee!'.

Rat and Mole spent most of the day at Badger's, who had invited the chief weasel to go over the coming night's event in order to ensure that everything went like clockwork. Mole was not at all comfortable in the presence of a weasel, but as his friends were here he felt safe enough.

Badger said to the chief weasel, "My friends and I would like to be present at Toad Hall when the fun starts, only as observers, you understand. We will take no part in the proceedings, in fact you will hardly notice us at all." The weasel nodded and shook hands with us all, then left to rally his troops.

Rat and Mole also took their leave after arranging to meet Badger at the bridge in an hour's time.

Meanwhile, at Toad Hall, Toad avoided Florence as much as possible, spending a good deal of the time in his room, playing patience and only coming out for his meals, which were eaten in silence.

But as she rose from the table, she grunted at him, "Don't forget to get that key cut, Toad," before going back up to her room. Toad lay on the bed fully clothed; he wanted to be ready for anything. Sometime later he heard her come out of her room and go down to the kitchen for her nightly glass of hot milk, and on returning slammed her door shut.

Toad looked out of the window. It was beginning to get dark. *Now let the show begin*, thought Toad, and his excitement rose to fever pitch. He took another look out of the window. It was now quite dark, and he thought he saw movement at the back of the house, but he couldn't be certain.

At the appointed time Rat and Mole met Badger at the bridge. They were equipped with flasks of hot drinks and warm rugs to sustain them through their vigil. They made their way in the darkness to Toad Hall and took up their position in the shrubbery close to the house, which would afford them a good view of the proceedings without being seen. They had not been there long before they heard low voices and saw small, shadowy figures huddled against the wall of the house beneath the windows. They looked at each other and smiled.

Inside the house, all was quiet. Toad lay on his bed, all expectant. He didn't have long to wait.

"Eek! Eek!" came the awful scream from the room next door, followed by, "Toad, come quick!"

Toad, who could hardly contain his glee, went to her door and was met by a distraught Florence.

"There were things over there by the window, horrible faces staring at me. Do something,

Toad, do something."

He went to the window, opened it and looked out. He saw two figures huddled on the floor of the balcony, who grinned up at him. He winked back at them before closing the window.

"There is nobody there, Florence," he said.

"But they were there, Toad, they really were," she said.

"Well if they were, they have gone now." He suggested she went back to bed, then he said goodnight and went back to his own room. He flung himself on his bed and laughed out loud.

He was ecstatic.

Within a quarter of an hour the scream came again, louder this time. She hammered on Toad's door, shouting, "Toad, they're back, I can't stand any more of this. I am going to sleep on the sofa downstairs."

Toad opened his door to see her going down the stairs, carrying a blanket from her bed. Toad suspected that the night's events were not over yet and he was right. The weasels must have heard what she planned to do and acted accordingly. They gave her about fifteen minutes to get settled on the sofa, then started again, this time on the ground floor. When the screaming started yet again, Toad could no longer contain himself and burst into uncontrolled laughter, and though he hadn't slept all night, he was delighted.

The weasels' activities continued for another hour, then silence. Toad waited for half an hour, then ventured downstairs, and found Florence huddled in the corner of the kitchen, and he suddenly felt sorry for her. Taking her by the arm, he led her into the lounge and gave her a glass of brandy. By now the party was over and the weasels had gone, so Toad helped Florence up to her room.

It was past midday when Florence made an appearance down to the kitchen, where Toad was preparing some lunch.

She said to Toad in a quiet voice, "They were really out there, Toad, why won't you believe me?"

Toad replied, "I didn't see or hear anything, I don't understand it."

Florence then said, "Well I am not staying to find out. I'm leaving today." She then returned to her room and made her preparations to leave.

It was now daylight, and although Toad had sacrificed a night's sleep, he did not feel overtired. He poured himself a drink and congratulated himself on the success of the previous night's venture. Florence's cases were ready by the front door, and she had already telephoned for a taxi.

Toad thought he would pay Rat and Mole a visit, but when he got to the front door, he saw the taxi coming up the drive, so he waited. Florence was coming down the stairs, having seen the taxi arrive, and with the help of Toad and the driver, her cases were put on board. Then without so much as a goodbye, she climbed into the taxi and was gone.

Toad set out for Rat's house, and as he crossed the bridge, he saw Badger coming down the path from Wild Wood, and waited for him to catch up.

"Hello Badger," he said.

And Badger replied, "Hello, Toad, what did you think of the show last night?"

Toad said that it was wonderful, and added, "That plan of yours, Badger, was a masterpiece." Badger told Toad it was the weasels he should be thanking, as they had done all the work.

As the two friends walked along the path towards Rat's house, they laughed together at some of the more hilarious moments of last night's escapade. As they approached Rat's house, they saw them both sitting on the veranda.

"Hello you two," they called out, and they waved in reply.

Rat said, "Come in and we can all share the joke."

Badger laughed as he explained to them how he and Toad were reliving some of the funniest moments from the escapade the night before. "You have to admit though, Rattie, that at times, it was quite hilarious," said Toad, and Rat laughed and said, "I can't argue with that," then Badger commented, "well all's well that ends well, at least she's gone."

"Good riddance," said Toad.

Mole prepared a special meal for them all to celebrate the evening. Everyone was in high spirits and the atmosphere was most jovial as they discussed the most amusing aspects of the night before. Badger, Rat and Mole listened avidly to Toad's account of the reaction of Florence to the antics of the weasels, which made them all laugh loudly.

When the meal was eventually over, Rat and Mole cleared the table and they went into the lounge, where Rat produced a decanter and some glasses.

He held up the decanter and said, "This is a fine brandy that I have been saving for a special occasion, such as this one," then he poured a generous measure into each glass and handed them round. Then he raised his glass and said, "Here's to the four of us, may we always remain good friends."

The others responded likewise, saying solemnly, "The four of us."

Toad said that it was time for him to say a few words. He stood up and said, "My friends, I can't thank you enough for what you did, and the weasels of course, and I owe you all a debt I

can never repay, but I thank you from the bottom of my heart."

Badger replied, "That is what friends are for, Toad."

Toad then said, "I am thinking of holding a small gathering at the Hall, and inviting the weasels to attend. It goes without saying that you three are invited too, and it will give me the opportunity to formally thank them for their participation."

Rat said, "Are you sure that is wise, Toad? There is no need to overdo it."

Toad replied, "Not the whole tribe, just those that took part – and the chief, of course."

The weasels soon received their payment, and Badger delivered Toad's invitation to the chief weasel, which was very well received. When the day of Toad's party arrived, Rat, Mole and Badger turned up at Toad Hall to find that six of the weasels plus their chief had already arrived, and surprisingly had taken some trouble towards looking respectable. They were all shown into the dining room where the table was already prepared.

Food and drink was there in abundance, and they all took their places and waited for Toad to address them.

Toad got to his feet and looked round at the table at their expectant faces, then he said, "My good friends, my heartfelt thanks to you all for your noble efforts on my behalf. As a consequence, I would hope that our future relationship will improve." Then he raised his glass and said, "Your health, gentlemen," and the feasting began. It is an odd thing that from that day, Mole seemed to lose his fear of Wild Wood.

CPSIA information can be obtained
at www.ICGtesting.com
Printed in the USA
BVIC01n0121110717
489032BV00009B/33

* 9 7 8 1 5 0 2 7 8 5 9 0 9 *